First published 1982 by Abelard-Schuman Ltd
Text and illustrations © Rod Campbell 1982, 2007
This edition first published 2009 by Campbell Books
an imprint of Macmillan Children's Books
a division of Macmillan Publishers Ltd
20 New Wharf Road, London N1 9RR
Basingstoke and Oxford
www.panmacmillan.com
Associated companies worldwide
ISBN 978-0-230-70953-9
Printed in Malaysia
9 8 7 6 5 4 3 2 1

Dear Zoo

Rod Campbell

Campbell Books

I wrote to the zoo
to send me a pet.
They sent me an...

He was too big!
I sent him back.

So they sent me a...

He was too tall!
I sent him back.

So they sent me a…

He was too fierce!
I sent him back.

So they sent me a...

He was too scary!
I sent him back.

So they sent me a...

He was too naughty!
I sent him back.

So they sent me a…

He was too jumpy!
I sent him back.

So they thought
very hard, and
sent me a...

He was perfect!
I kept him.

He was too grumpy!
I sent him back.

So they sent me a…